THE FAIRIES OF FERRY BEACH

and Other Stories

(Stories for All Ages)

by Connie Dunn

The Fairies of Ferry Beach: and Other Stories © 2013 Connie Dunn

Published by Nature Woman Wisdom Press

First Edition. Printed and bound in the United States of America.

Copyright © 2013 Connie Dunn
ISBN-13: 978-0615747705

Published by Nature Woman Wisdom
Printed in The United States of America

January, 2013
9 8 7 6 5 4 3 2

Library of Congress Cataloging in Publication Data

Dunn, Connie
The Fairies of Ferry Beach: and Other Stories

Ferry Beach
The Fairies of Ferry Beach: and Other Stories
by Connie Dunn

Spiritual
The Fairies of Ferry Beach: and Other Stories Told
by Connie Dunn

Stories
The Fairies of Ferry Beach: and Other Stories
by Connie Dunn

for all the people – young and old – that love Ferry Beach

for my daughter, Michelle, who edits my work

for my daughter, Erin, who knows Ferry Beach

for my wife, Joyce, who is a Life Member of Ferry Beach

for my loving friends at Ferry Beach

for all the people, whose spirit has come to the sea

*for first-time Ferry Beachers and
seasoned Ferry Beachers, as well*

4

LIFE MEMBER QUOTES FROM 2012 LIFE MEMBER BANQUET

"Ferry Beach helps people learn values that matter, learn how to put beliefs in action, learn how to clarify what is important."

"It is a place where we make plans for change and social justice."

"It is a place which opens spiritual windows for us as well as doors into new areas of personal development."

"Acceptance of diversity, skills to work in a group using positive energy, ways to think outside of the box."

"Opportunities for meaningful spiritual connections with a wide variety of like-minded, like hearted persons."

"A comfortable safe environment to share with people who become friends and share ideas and plans."

"An intentional community which creates spaces for people to connect with one another, with new ideas and experiences and with the natural world - and to grow in wisdom and spirit and take it out into the world."

"Love, connection, community, friends, safety, acceptance of diversity, fun laughter, new ideas, singing, nature, the beach, the Grove, a place to be yourself."

TABLE OF CONTENTS

CHURCH SEEDS:

a Quillen Shinn Story

"Scoundrels!" he bellowed. "They are wolves in sheep's clothing with the intent of deceiving our soul-worthy members! A minister must be not only pure in heart but loyal to his faith and exhibit good common sense if he is to win souls for the kingdom (of God), Doctor Reverend Quillen Hamilton Shinn remarked sternly.

Doctor Reverend Quillen Hamilton Shinn was intolerant of ministers who were not honest, virtuous, moral, and loyal Universalists. He was known to be vocal about this topic. For example, Shinn was on his way to Canton Theology School at St. Lawrence University, but decided to stop in at the Universalist General Convention that was being held in Baltimore. As he arrived, a heated debate became so volatile that it upset Shinn; he broke protocol by speaking without being recognized. He chastised the delegates telling them that he was on his way to seminary, but he was tempted to change his plans and return home, because of their behavior. He added that "Universalist ministers write better than they speak." His words changed the bedlam into a "love feast."

THE MINISTER AT TWENTY-FIVE.

For those born on New Year's Day, expectations and destinies are often speculated. Quillen Shinn was born on the first day of 1845. Some people claimed that he was born a missionary, which spoke more for Shinn's abilities and convictions than reality. However, he did begin his missionary work early in his career. Of course, he was only 25, when he became ordained.

It was a good time to be a missionary, because Universalism was in its formative years. Universalist Churches were not common in most states. Therefore, being a missionary brought travel. In the 1870s, travel was mostly by horse or horse and carriage.

For Shinn, who was not a wealthy man, his missionary work was done by horseback, riding from town to town ministering and speaking to small groups gathered in someone's home or tent or some location that could accommodate the group that gathered. They called these horseback riding missionaries, circuit riders, because they traveled around in a certain territory. Shinn rode his circuit, and as he did, he sowed *Church* seeds.

"You can never plant anything, and set it growing without organization," Shinn said. Wherever he found interest, he would start a Sunday school, youth group, ladies' aid group or worship services. These were the seeds of churches, which Shinn found at the heart of his missionary work. He didn't have a set formula, but used the energy generated within a few people to sprout more interest and grow the group into a church.

His enthusiasm was catching! "Why not organize Sunday schools all over the land, in every town, city, hamlet and country place, where live two or more families of our faith? We ought to start a thousand Sunday Schools at once!" he proclaimed!

Although Shinn gave it a good try sowing seeds in a thousand or more places, his reported count was only sixty organized churches. There were, of course, countless other groups that never quite grew into a church during his missionary tenure. It certainly wasn't for lack of trying that kept Shinn for organizing more churches. In less than three years, Shinn traveled more than 15,000 miles, averaging almost one sermon a day. He covered 34 states, the District of Columbia, and two Canadian provinces in his circuit. Because he made so many stops in his travels and his visits were so brief, he was often called the "Grasshopper Missionary." It did not deter Shinn. He continued his work diligently.

Shinn had his missionary work fine-tuned, but not regimented. Whenever he could gather two families or more, he started with smaller groups like Sunday school and youth groups,. When interest warranted, however, he would select a leader to organize a building fund. Shinn would find them a part-time minister and help them raise the money. Shinn's claim to fame was fundraising; he raised more money for distinctly Universalist Mission work than any other Universalist minister.

While his preaching was very conservative and Bible-based, he had very progressive ideas, which extended to fundraising. For one of his churches, he asked people to put boxes on their mantles and put pennies into it each day. At another, he sold names for ten cents a name and had them added to a quilt.

While neither a penny or ten cents seem like much money in the 21st century, in the late 19th century, which is more than one hundred years ago, an average family earned around $2.50 a day. Today (2012), that same family would earn $150 a day. To be equal to a penny a day, a family would need to put away $3.75 into their box on the mantle to equal that each day. The families would have to pay $37.50 per name to get their names on that fundraising quilt to be equal to the ten cents in the late 1800s.

Shinn had been appointed the General Missionary for the Universalists. At that time, the groves in summer became the Universalists' sanctuaries. There were gatherings in various parts of the country, including in the prairies where families came in covered wagons. Shinn discovered the enchantment and missionary power of summer gatherings in 1881 in New Hampshire. It was an opportunity for families to hear an array of sermons from many noted Universalist preachers. He also saw the potential for promoting denominational life as a whole and an extension of Universalist missionary work. Shinn also found it as an opportune time for raising funds for mission work.

The experience of the summer meetings so moved and excited Shinn that later that same (1881) summer, he attended the Unitarian summer meeting, at The Weirs, located on Lake Winnipesaukee, New Hampshire. Upon leaving the meeting, he told his wife, "I am going to hold a meeting here next year, and I will get a thousand people to attend."

The next year, Shinn arranged to use The Weirs, a Methodist-owned facility. He arranged lodging for folks at hotels, boarding houses, and farmhouses. He had arranged for speakers and musicians. He even contracted with the railroad to bring folks to the area. Lastly, he named the event: *The National Universalist Grove Meeting.-*

The *Grove Meetings* were moved in 1897 to Sarasota, New York, to give Shinn time to look for a more permanent location. By 1901, Shinn had discovered the beautiful and magical grounds on the Atlantic Coast at Ferry Beach in Maine. Twenty-five years from their first Summer Grove meeting in New Hampshire, The Ferry Beach Park Association was formed. This *Grove Meeting* occupied the property as guests of the Boston and Maine Railroad, owners of the property. Shinn began his fundraising efforts immediately, so that they could purchase the property. The Ferry Beach House, a hotel, was purchased from the railroad in 1904, which is now Quillen. Other parts of Ferry Beach were slowly added after Shinn's death in 1907 (see brief history of those changes below in Ferry Beach Park Association History).

Reverend Quillen Hamilton Shinn and his Universalist spirit live on at Ferry Beach. He believed that "God is love" and that "there is no hell for any of us to fear, outside of ourselves." Many changes to Universalism, as an organized religion have changed, including its merger with Unitarianism to form what is now known as the Unitarian Universalist Association and its numerous church members all across the nation. Ferry Beach is a treasured Unitarian Universalist retreat and conference center. If this is your first visit, here's hoping it won't be your last!

Ferry Beach Park
Association History

according to Ferry Beach

In 1911, a house was built behind Quillen and named in honor of Carrie P. Underwood, a benefactor of the Beach. The Grove, which is now the Chapel in the Grove, was purchased from the railroad in 1916. A few years later, an Annex was built onto Quillen. Rowland Hall was built in 1927 and named in honor of Dr. William R. Rowland, president of the Association from 1919 until his death in 1925.

Across from Quillen in 1945, a house was purchased and named Claflin Cottage in honor of Edward P. Claflin, a former board member and a benefactor of the Beach. The next year, Gardiner Cottage was purchased and named in honor of

Marion L. Gardiner who bequeathed funds for its purchase. The Rose Pavilion was built in the Grove in 1975, which was named in honor of William Wallace Rose, minister of the Lynn (MA) Universalist church for 30 years. The Quillen Lobby was remodeled in 1976 and dedicated to Edward Hempel, longtime treasurer and Executive Secretary of the Ferry Park Association. In 1979, the sand dunes restoration project was begun.

A Capital Fund Drive was held from 1986 to 2001, which allowed the Beach to purchase Manning Cottage, which was named for Robert Manning. It was sold shortly afterwards. The Dining Room in Quillen was built in 1990 and named in honor of the Rev. Earle Dolphin, who was a long-time Ferry Beacher and resident musician. The Health Center and Children's Room were also relocated and renovated the same year. Sewer connections were completed for all the buildings and Grove sites, as well. Plus, the Stone Environmental School began renting the property in the off-season.

Between 1995 and 2003, Rowland Hall was remodeled and other major improvements were completed to meet fire codes. The Ferry Beach Ecology School was begun in 1998. During 2002 and 2003, Quillen was remodeled from top to bottom, including accessible bathrooms and a new lobby. A new store was built onto the side of Claflin in 2003. More improvements were made in 2004, which included the Memorial Garden, the building of Kelly Cottage, which was built as a "green" building. It was the first new building built at Ferry Beach in over 30 years.

New playground equipment was installed in 2004 and 2005. A new handicapped accessible bathroom was built in Underwood in 2005, as well as having the tennis-basketball court renovated. Both Grove wash houses were also remodeled.

In 2006, the Eleanor B. Forbes Chapel in the Grove was renovated thanks to a generous donation. Handicapped accessible ramps and walkways were installed at both Underwood and Gardiner. The next year brought in the remodeling of the Rowland Auditorium, which was renamed "The GAYLA Theatre," because the GAYLA camp sponsored the remodeling.

GAYLA is the gay men's and male supporters' camp. At the time GAYLA was formed at Ferry Beach, it was one of the only places that Gay men could be out and be totally supported and validated. Similarly, the Sappho's Sisters was a Lesbian group that also was one of the only places that Lesbian women could be out and totally supported and validated. This group was rolled into the *In the Company of Women* camp, which brought in diverse group of women.

The 2nd Century Fund Capital Campaign raised money for several projects including building a new Dining Hall. In 2009, improvements began with fortifying the dunes, which had been devastated during a big storm that wiped out some houses down the street from Quillen. Next, Rowland Hall dormitory spaces were upgraded and insulated. Then, site excavation and foundation work was begun for the new Metz Village, the Nurse's Cabin, and the Dining Hall. In 2011, both the Metz Village and the DeWolfe Dining Facility were completed and the Nurse's cabin was settled onto its new foundation.

ONCE UPON A PENNY KINGDOM

written at Ferry Beach, 2009

Once upon a Penny Kingdom, there lived a queen, named Goldie. And in this kingdom, everything gold was hers. She liked having gold around her so much that she had golden plates and goblets; golden forks and spoons. She wore only jewels mounted in gold, because this is what she liked.

And that was the way the Penny Kingdom was for many, many years. But alas, poor Goldie ordered golden cloth. The smelters came and melted the gold and the spinners came and spun the gold into cloth. Then, the tailors took the cloth and many of her jewels to sew it into the most beautiful gown that anyone had ever seen. At least that's what the tailors promised.

One tailor's name was Greenlee and the other Goldenrod, but they were not so honest and stole the golden cloth. While Goldie was beside herself, she had not thought what it meant for her kingdom. With the gold gone, the peasants soon learned how it affected them.

Queen Goldie could not pay the knights that guarded her palace. She could not buy the food to feed the horses. She could not buy the food for any of the feasts. Queen Goldie was broke and had nothing to spend.

Queen Goldie had to ask the peasants to pay for everything. And since she basically had no money or anything to trade for goods she needed, she decided to call in her magicians.

Onesuch Magician came to her and told the Queen he had a magic wand that could help her. "But," he said, "you must turn your palace over to the people, so that they have ownership in their Queen's problem. Queen Goldie thought about it a minute or two and agreed to the terms of Onesuch.

Onesuch called all the peasants to the palace and held her wand over an ordinary brick as she said some powerful magical words. "Aaank!" went the wand. Onesuch got an idea, but again the wand went: "Aaank!" And nothing happened.

This time, Onesuch asked the peasants for magical words, someone said "Peanut Butter." But the wand went "Aaank!" And nothing happened.

Onesuch tried again, "What word would you suggest?" ________________ (wait for audience to give words). But each time, Onesuch held the wand, the wand went "Aaank!"

Onesuch decided to try one last time, and this time a peasant child with a face like an angel looked up into Onesuch's eyes and said, "please."

Queen Goldie said, "Please is not a magic word. It's polite, but not magic!"

Onesuch shrugged her shoulders and said, perhaps we should try it. She held the magic wand over the brick and said the word: please. "Aaank!" went the wand.

The same sweet child went up to Onesuch and whispered, "You haven't used the magic word correctly."

Now Onesuch had been a magician for a number of years, and clearly had not faced this outcome. She was surprised. "Tell me what have I done wrong?" Onesuch asked.

The child smiled again, even wider. She whispered into Onesuch's ear, you've got to ask your question to the people not the brick."

"Ahhhhh," Onesuch said, "Like this?"

So Onesuch said, "Friends and residents of Penny Kingdom, I beg of you to help Queen Goldie. She needs you to support the palace. Dig deep into the bottoms of your pockets and give all the money you can."

Then, he started to swish the wand over the heads of the crowd. But as he looked down at the angelic child and other children...he said, "I think I need your help!"

So all the children said: "PLEASE!" And the wand went "BLING!"

The peasants came orderly streaming up the palace aisle and gave their money to the Queen. And the Penny Kingdom was saved. Queen Goldie never ever asked for frivolous things again, because she always remembered how hard the people worked to help the kingdom do the work of the kingdom.

Queen Goldie went before the kingdom and said, "a penny saved is a penny earned! We will make our kingdom great again."

And so they did a penny and a dime at a time!

AUNTIE TWIT AND THE TEXAS MOSQUITOES

a tall Texas tale told at Ferry Beach 2010

One evening Auntie (pronounced Ant-tee) Twit was walkin' down her favorite path in the woods when she came face to face with a pack of Mosquitoes. Yep, you heard right: a pack. You see, in Texas everything is a lot bigger, including Mosquitoes or 'Skeeters,' as some folks call 'em.

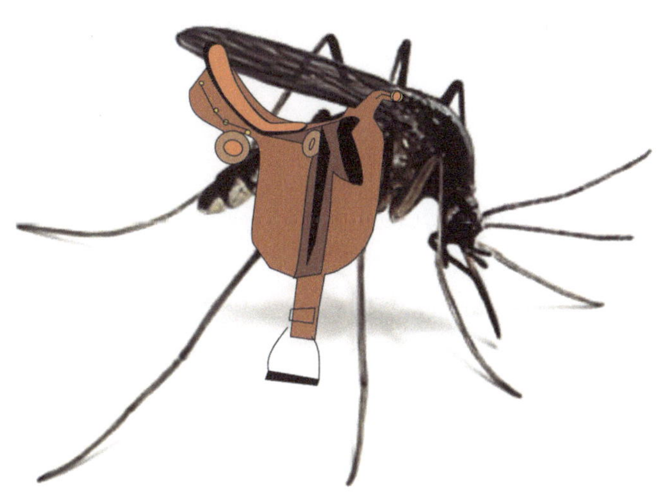

Why these 'Skeeters were big enough to saddle and ride. In the West…uh I mean the Western part of Texas, they even have Mosquito Rodeos. One hotshot riding a Wild 'Skeeter got thrown clean over the fence. And then some folks driving down the freeway wrecked their car when a pack of Mosquitoes ran out in front of them. The car was totaled. Luckily, they only had minor injuries.

These Texas-sized 'Skeeters were so big that strappin' a saddle on 'em and riding 'em like a Stallion works fairly well. Of course, Stallions are pretty smart; I can't say the same about 'Skeeters. They are so enormous that they cannot sting or fly, which means that they aren't as much of a nuisance. These are the sorts of whopping huge Mosquitoes that Auntie Twit faced.

Now, Auntie Twit was known for taking nothin' from no-one or no-thing. So, it isn't surprising that, Auntie Twit yelled at the creatures, "Move your ugly beaks out of my way!"

The 'Skeeters returned a buzz that was so loud it was more roar than buzz. Auntie Twit was not daunted and stood her ground. But Auntie Twit did not turn back and return down the path from which she had come from. Instead, she widened her stance and waited for the ugly 'Skeeters to make their move.

As she stood her ground, she wondered if 'Skeeter Stew really tasted like chicken. Then, she realized that these monstrous 'Skeeters would be a heavy lot to haul. Since she always carried her walking stick when she walked, she began to plan her strategy for gettin' past these creatures.

Well, the ugly beasts wouldn't budge or move off the trail, so Auntie Twit took her walking stick and whapped the mosquitos' beaks hard. Once, then twice!

When Auntie Twit hit them on their beaks for the third time it made the monster mosquitoes stop in their tracks. However, these ogres were persistent. They might not be able to sting at their size, but their colossal size made them a menacing adversary. There had been reports that they consumed small animals. Who knew if they had moved up to humans?

Auntie Twit was a tiny woman at a four-foot, eleven-inches in height. These Wild 'Skeeters were bigger than Auntie Twit by at least a foot. But though she was a small-framed, small-statured woman, she had no fear of just about anything. She had gone skydiving on her 68th birthday, SCUBA diving on her 69th, and bungee jumping on her 70th. In response, Auntie Twit said: "We're all going to die sometime. I might as well live a little now! I might be dead, later!"

With this sort of courage, Auntie Twit hit the 'Skeeters a fourth time hard across their beaks, but still they didn't run away and continued to block the trail. They were in a standoff. Auntie Twit needed a different approach.

Auntie Twit backed up a little and came running at the beasts. Just before she actually reached the fiends, she used her walkin' stick to pole vault over this menacing pack.

The pack of 'Skeeters did an about-face and watched Auntie Twit walk on down the trail. Auntie Twit did not look behind her. Had she done so, she would have seen these ballooned-up creatures pursuing her.

She must have felt them coming, because she stopped suddenly and turned around to see the 'Skeeters still in pursuit. She thought quickly, then took her stick and held it like a spear. 'Skeeter One ran full-speed into the walkin' stick, which pierced the critter through and through! The other two 'Skeeters kept on coming; and Auntie Twit turned her walking stick toward 'Skeeter two. He also was skewered. The third one was still barreling toward her. She moved her walking stick toward the third one, which was difficult because of the weight of the two previous 'Skeeters.

Wouldn't you know it, the last foolish and immense monster, skewered itself on her walking stick?

Auntie Twit had lost her enthusiasm for her walk and had gotten a pretty good workout, so she returned home, barbecued the 'Skeeters, and lived to tell the tale.

Now...the next time you're in Texas, take your walkin' stick out with you into the woods in case you run into a pack of 'Skeeters!

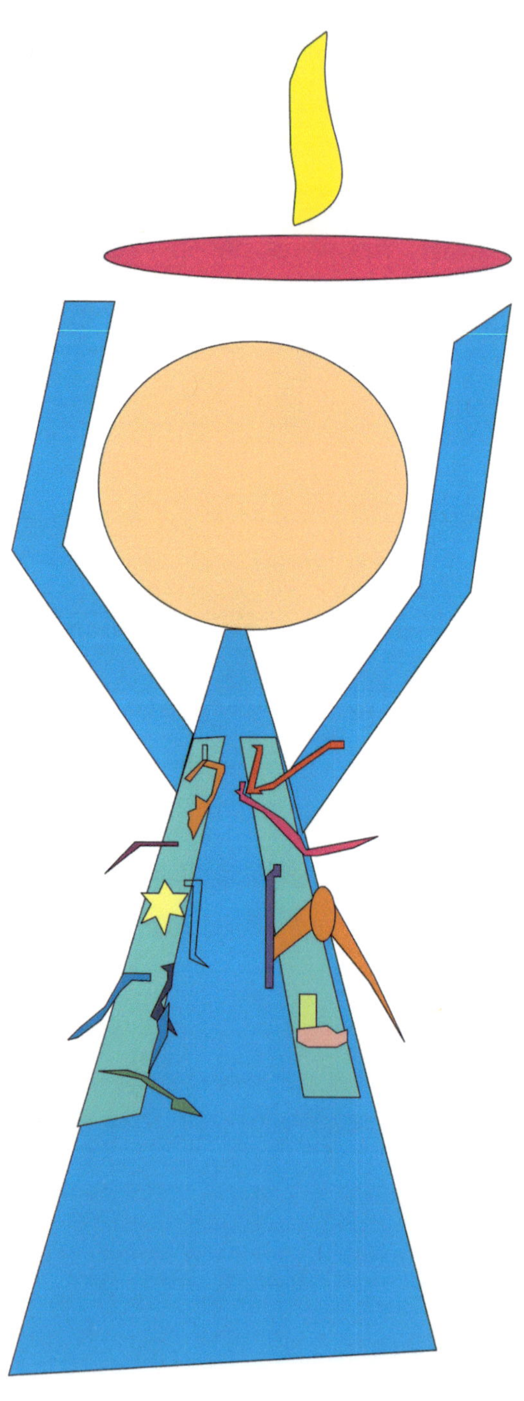

THE TATTERED STOLE

(written for Ferry Beach at Ferry Beach, Summer, 2008)

A Ferry Beach Story

There once was or was not a Director of Religious Education who attended Ferry Beach, a Unitarian Universalist conference center and camp in Maine near Saco. Every year, she would come and be with the children and youth, because that's what she loved to do.

As was her practice, she would tell stories and when she told her stories, she would put on a storyt--elling stole. But as the years wore on, many of her stoles became tattered and worn. She treasured the stoles, because in each of them were the memories of the years she had spent at Ferry Beach.

One year, she met another person at Ferry Beach, who took all her stoles and made them into one. Carefully, the fabric artist cut away all the bad pieces and created a wonderful stole, making sure the sparkle star and the crayon wrapped in gymp were all part of the new stole. This was of great importance to her, because these were gifts from the children for which she told stories.

The next year, the woman was thrilled to wear her new stole as she told stories to the children and youth. But as it happens, years passed and the same stole made from many tattered stoles became shabby and worn. And as it also happens, the woman, too, was getting old like her stole. She found that she could no longer come to Ferry Beach and tell the stories to the children and youth that made her soul smile. But like so many things that are precious, she could not let go of the *Tattered Stole*. Instead, the woman found someone, much like she had been, who could carry on the tradition of telling the stories to the children and youth.

And so, as I tell you this story, I proudly wear this *Tattered Stole*. And I will tell you that the first time I wore this stole, a child asked me why I put rags around my neck. I told the child about the wonderful woman who came to Ferry Beach each summer and told stories to children and youth. I told her about the sparkly star that some child or youth gave to the woman and about the crayon that still hangs from the stole, still wrapped in gymp.

"But why do you wear it?" asked the child.

I answered, "Because this *Tattered Stole* carries the memories of Ferry Beach. It holds all the memories of the woman who first wore it…and now my memories. And as you leave Ferry Beach this summer, I hope you carry the memories of friends and staff in something like a rock, a shell, a friendship bracelet, or something else. That way, you, too, will hold all the memories from the *Tattered Stole* of songs sung, art projects, games, the beach, the sand, the ocean, and all the stories told here while you were at Ferry Beach this year.

And when you are older, I hope you, too, will be the one that passes on the stories and wears this *Tattered Stole*.

The child smiled a big smile; and somehow the woman knew that in a few years, she would pass on the tattered storytelling stole to this child.

THE FAIRIES AT FERRY BEACH

true story from events at Ferry Beach, 2012

Once upon a weekend, there were fairies entered into the yearly Banathalon at Ferry Beach. Now, I'm sure you've heard tell' that fairies live under trees and bushes. But these fairies were visitors to Ferry Beach, a Unitarian Universalist camp and conference center in Saco, Maine, which sits on the Atlantic seaboard.

This group of fairies looked fairly normal, as normal as folks come at Ferry Beach. They were of normal size, including the wee ones: Alyssa, Kyleigh, and Abigail. Their ears were less pointy than I would have imagined for fairies, but true enough, these fairies had wings. Okay, so they were mostly cardboard covered in satin and decorated with gems and leaves and other natural items, but fairies in all their mythical fiber.

Magic is in abundance at Ferry Beach and comes in many flavors. The art room magic was definitely in effect when I first met the fairies. They were in full swing creative mode. The youngest of them, made a magic ring for me. Fairy rings and magic? What else could you ask for? And Alyssa, Kyleigh, and Abigail were the sweetest fairies, as well. They helped each other, and Joy, the grandmother of Alyssa and Kyleigh helped each of them when they asked for help. Otherwise, there were very happy crafting fairies!

As teams go for the Banathalon, the fairies may have been at a disadvantage. The wee ones took on the tasks of walking, riding a wheeled instrument (bicycle, in this case), and swimming around the buoy. The tall one, Joy, ate the banana after it had been passed from each little fairy and had finally landed in her hand, slightly smushed, but unpeeled, and ready for consumption.

She peeled and ate the banana. And the girls on her team screamed, squealed, and yelled out their happiness. The crowd cheered the eater along as well! So, when the banana was down, the next team was up. So the Banathalon proceeded!

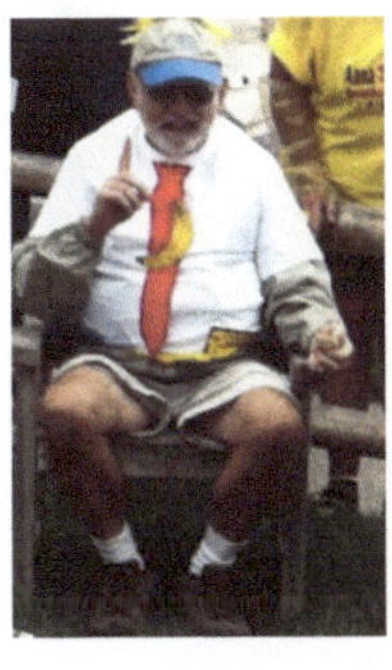

You may be wondering what a Banathalon is? If you did not catch the resemblance of a triathlon, then I should tell you that it is. However, instead of a baton to pass to team members, a banana is used. How long has Ferry Beach had Banathalons? Good question! Years! Perhaps a decade or so was as close of an answer that I got, but then there are a group of women who claim to be the past winners that date back to the 1940s. Yet again, these women aren't quite old enough to have been at Ferry Beach and entered into a Banathalon, but that's probably another story for another day.

While there are prizes for the Banathalon, it is more the fun of making costumes, and naming teams, and doing all the rest of the hoopla that surrounds the Banathalon that makes this team event so popular. All the participants usually get a prize: a teeny tiny (a very small ice cream cone) at the Ferry Beach store. The top winners, who are not necessarily the fastest because style is a large factor in the winning, are given t-shirts along with a certificate.

The Fairies at Ferry Beach could have won on cuteness, but there was a lot of competition. They participated in grace, and although they weren't the announced winners, they were all happy just to have participated and used their own-designed wings. Besides, a teeny tiny (very small ice cream cone) is a Ferry Beach tradition! Every participant gets a teeny tiny.

I have it on good authority that the Fairies may return to Ferry Beach. Of course, there are a lot of camps to choose from. So, if you want to catch them, you'll have to look for them at all the camps.

When does the annual Banathalon happen? In the past, it has always happened on Labor Day weekend. However, Gail Forsythe Vail and her husband, Stephen, have coordinated this weekend and organized the Banathalon for quite a few years. The 2012 Labor Day was their final weekend to coordinate; they were passing on the leadership.

Will 2012 be the last Banathalon? Probably not! It's way too much fun for it to disappear into Ferry Beach history. It may crop up somewhere else in another camp. For now, the Banathalon is put on hold. Whenever you find it or create it, yourself, look for the fairies. They won't be too far away!

THE MERFOLK DREAMS

written at Ferry Beach 2010

Standing on the beach watching the waves roll in, I noticed something in the water. It was just after daybreak, so almost none of the campers were awake yet. However, *the something in the water*, became more clearly a body.

Finally, I could see that there was definitely a body: the body of a Mermaid. She came up close, waved, and dived back into the waves. It happened so quickly, I wondered if it had happened at all. Was it that I truly wanted to see a Mermaid? Ah, the questions that I had that morning on the beach. But I finally gave into what I had seen: a mermaid.

Now, folks at Ferry Beach have been dreaming about Mermaids and Mermen for over a hundred years. When you get all snuggled in your bed and lie quiet, you can hear the ocean waves splashing on the beach. This nice rhythmic sound of crashing waves or gentle laps can lull you to sleep. Perhaps, it is the ocean waves that bring the Merfolk into your dreams? Perhaps, it is the Merfolk who make you more aware of the ocean sounds, so that they can come into your dreams. Whatever brings them to you, you can be sure that you were meant to go with them on some adventure or the other.

They can take you down in the ocean on a dreamy coral reef, where all the bright colored fish swim in and out of the coral, seaweed, and other ocean plants. You can see how alive the bottom of the ocean is. The sea has a way of using many things that are dumped into it. A sunken ship becomes a habitat for many types of creatures, such as barnacles, sea urchins and schools of various fish.

You might see yourself playing hide and seek with the fish or maybe view a very large fish at a safe distance. The Merfolk will keep you out of harm's way and safely return you to your bed. They just guide you through your dream journey in the ocean.

The night after I saw the Mermaid, I was anxious to go to sleep and see if she would come to me in my dreams. Sure enough! She came to me in my dreams and took me on the most wonderful adventure. Before your adventures start, however, you have to close your eyes and lie quietly.

Listen to the waves. Let them rock you to sleep. Hear the lullaby of the deep flowing sea, as it rocks you ever so gently. The seaweed wraps you to keep you warm, and the Merfolk tell you stories.

My Mermaid called to me in my dreams. Outside my Ferry Beach room, the wind blew lightly through the leaves, and the clear rolling waves filled my head. She took me down in the deep sea where the -octopus lives with its eight legs and the whales travel on their paths. She showed me a cave where the Merfolk live with their children. I saw the MerChildren's collections of shells and trinkets that they've found along the ocean floor.

I took a ride on a sea turtle, and then suddenly I found myself in my Ferry Beach bed wrapped warmly in my sleeping bag. Now, I'm sure there are some of you who will doubt that I ever saw a Mermaid, but that's okay. There are yet others who will understand, because they, too, have had Merfolk Dreams.

BILLY, THE WHALE

as told at Ferry Beach 2010

One year, Billy, the whale, came to Ferry Beach. He was registered in the *Kids for the Earth* camp.

He was so excited as he packed his backpack full storage under the Great Coral Reef he got so excited that his mother had to give him a few time outs to get him calm enough to travel.

Now, Billy wasn't your ordinary camper, of course, but when you come to Ferry Beach, you expect that. While diversity is embraced at Ferry Beach, perhaps no one was quite ready for Billy. There is question even today that he probably wasn't ready to come to camp, but I'm sure that doesn't apply to anyone reading or hearing this story!

We all know that the first things you have to learn at camp are the rules, but Billy might not have listened to them. He went pretty much anywhere he wanted to go, even into the kitchen and the girl's bathroom!

Billy didn't go to any workshops, because he kept missing them while he was exploring the campus. But someone...and you know who that someone is...one of the counselors had to go find him.

Billy just kept wandering off, which wasn't very safe. He even ended up in a *Different Drummers* workshop. He wasn't registered for that age group camp!

Usually, Billy didn't even come in off the playground when the dinner bell was rung. So...yep, you got it! A counselor had to go find him.

One day they found him eating ice cream during one of the workshop times. And everyone at the *Kids for the Earth Camp* know that NO ONE...I mean NO ONE...gets ice cream when it's not ice cream getting time!

When it was bedtime, Billy made so much noise that he kept everyone in camp awake. And we all know that when it's quiet time at Ferry Beach, no one is supposed to make noise.

The one thing that Billy was very good at was making friends. He liked everyone! In spite of all his rule-breaking, just about everyone, including counselors, liked Billy, as well.

On the day that camp was over, they all cried with Billy, the whale. It was Billy's first camp experience, and he was a bit sad to be leaving. All the other campers said it was the best camp ever, because Billy, the whale, was there. It helped them all remember their camp forever.

And well, they all cried, too, because it was the last day of camp. No more Teeny Tinies; no more beach time; no more art room adventures; and no more night time stories. Even the counselors cried!

But then they all hugged and promised to come back next year, including Billy, the Whale.

How many people do you know, who went to camp with a Whale?

THREE WISE UNITARIAN UNIVERSALISTS

written, 2003

Once upon a time not so very long ago, there were three wise or unwise Unitarian Universalists. The three were very good friends, but they often had different ideas, which caused them to be the best of adversaries, as well as friends.

On this particular day, the three were out taking a walk along the ocean. They were all at Ferry Beach for a weeklong workshop and were taking the opportunity for a nice long walk at sunrise. For those of you who don't know about Ferry Beach, it is a Unitarian Universalist camp on the Atlantic Ocean along the coast of Maine. At sunrise, the tide could be either at its peak or the highest level or at its lowest point.

When the three were walking, the Ocean was at low-tide level, which meant that more of the ocean floor could be viewed. This is a popular time to walk at Ferry Beach, because of the shells, rocks and driftwood that can be found.

The three came upon an object that they had never seen before. It stuck up through the sand, protruding upward like a roughly hewn obelisk or in more plain terms…it stuck up through the sand with a tall part pointed upward toward the sky. The three were also the only walkers at Ferry Beach that particular morning, because of the thick fog that hung over the ocean shore. It was so foggy that those that walked out on the platform toward the beach and looked out toward the ocean could just barely see the waves as they crested and met the shore. But these three Unitarian Universalist friends were die-hard walkers and were committed to walking even if it was pouring down rain. They might have balked had it been snowing. But since this was the middle of July, snow was not an issue. And other bad weather conditions, such as a hurricane, were also not on the horizon for this morning.

The oldest of these friends was Don. He had been a Unitarian Universalist minister for 20 years, and before that he had been a scientist. Don looked over the object very carefully, as any scientist would. He carefully ran his hand along one side and the top. He came to a conclusion and announced, "This object is an artifact from an ancient civilization. It was most likely used in their rituals as a sacred charm."

The next oldest of these Unitarian Universalists was Sophia. She was not a minister but instead was the director of religious education. She had been in this position at several churches over the last 18 years. And Sophia had become well known for her contributions of stories in which she prided herself. In fact, she often reminded people that she was following in Sophia Fahs' footsteps. Just so you know, Sophia Fahs was a pioneer in religious education and contributed a great deal to Unitarian Universalism through her retelling of many folktales and her curricula among other things.

Sophia had also been looking over the object they had found. She studied its peculiar markings and shape. She, too, ran her hand over the object. But she chose to encircle the object, touching it all the way around. Then, she boldly announced, "This is definitely no charm. I believe it is part of an old ship that has been encrusted in minerals over hundreds of years, which makes it appear more like a rock than wood. Actually, I think it may have been part of a carved wooden piece of a Viking ship that was most likely one of the ship's fittings."

The youngest of the Unitarian Universalist friends was Eric. He was a seminary student. He had known Don before he became a seminarian. He had met Sophia in his youth through his Young Religious Unitarian Universalist (YRUU) activities. And as he grew into adulthood, Eric had kept up his friendship. Don and Sophia had been colleagues working on UUA (Unitarian Universalist Association) committees.

Eric stood back and observed the object along with his observations of Don and Sophia. Unlike his elders, Eric was a bit hesitant. However, he carefully bent down and brushed the sand away from the object. As he lifted it out of its sandy home, he manipulated it in his hands. Again, he looked at his friends who were patiently waiting to hear his answer. A smirk came across his face, as he answered, "This is merely a rock, nothing more and nothing less."

Don insisted it was a sacred object and Sophia insisted even more that it was a valuable artifact from a Viking ship. Eric just stood and listened to the two argue for a while before he suggested that they take the object back to camp and form a committee to determine what it was. Don and Sophia shrugged and said, "Well, that's a good UU way to handle it!"

On the way back to camp, Don and Sophia asked Eric to define the objectives of the committee he had suggested. He answered that "the committee should be made up of experts from the ecology school that was housed at Ferry Beach."

Both Don and Sophia seemed happy with the makeup of the committee. However, they urged Eric to continue.

"Well," said Eric, "the experts should use all scientific means available to them to determine what this object is or more correctly what the object was before it landed on Ferry Beach."

Everyone seemed happy with the choice. And they immediately charged the newly found committee with that objective. But since the people who go to Ferry Beach for any weeklong event also become a very close community, the entire community was instantly fascinated with the trio's find. One of the organizers of the event at Ferry Beach suggested that each of the participants at Ferry Beach should write out what he or she thinks it is and put it in a suggestion box that materialized almost instantly.

The ecologists who suddenly found themselves with an unidentifiable object to identify did what most UU committees do: they met and talked and discussed their options.

By the end of the week, there was a lot of energy around what this object was that Sophia, Don and Eric had found. When the trio visited the committee to find out what they knew, they found that the committee was not able to discern what the object was any more than the three of them. Perhaps a bit disappointed that science did not solve their dilemma, they went to the organizers of the event to see how the participants voted.

There were 200 participants for the week with 150 who voted: 75 voted that the object was simply a rock; 25 said it was a sacred object; 26 thought it was part of an old Viking ship; and 24 said it was an alien from another planet. Keeping in the spirit of the community, the three agreed to present the results of the voting.

Don began, "It is truly an honor to be part of this community," he said. "About fifty of you don't know a rock from a piece of a ship or sacred object…so you abstained."

The community laughed. Sophia said, "But the good news is that a little more than a fourth of you had the imagination to see this object as a carved wooden piece that might have been a ship's fitting on a Viking Ship."

Again, the community laughed. Eric said, "But most of you saw the object as a rock, nothing more and nothing less. Perhaps, that means that most of you are practical."

Again, laughter came from the community. Then, Sophia said, "But most of all, there was another quarter of you that are severely warped and need immediate psychiatric attention!" Laughter filled the room.

"You all know who you are," said Don. "You are the ones that think what we found on the beach was an alien from another planet! I'll be in Quillen this evening for any of you who need counseling."

Again, laughter filled the hall. And the three friends hugged.

"You know," said the event organizer, "We all take home from Ferry Beach something valuable: some of you come for the relaxing week; some of you for the knowledge you would get in the workshops; and some of you come for the community. And I hope each of you found something special like Eric's rock, Don's sacred object and Sophia's piece of a Viking ship."

Don returned to the microphone and added, "But we're all right, you see!"

The room became totally silent. "The object is sacred; we all made it sacred this week. And Sophia's imagination made it unique and interesting just like one of her stories that she's been telling us for years. Eric's practical side of seeing this object as plainly a rock is simply like those of you who lean toward the humanist side and cannot wrap your soul around the idea of spirituality."

And so it was that at Ferry Beach near Saco, Maine, three wise Unitarian Universalists found an object that reminds us all that our perception of things often determines how we understand them.

WHO IS QUILLEN SHINN?

"Why do all the buildings have names?" asked Peter.

Carly smiled and said, "Because they're named after people."

"Quillen is a person?" Peter questioned in disbelief that anyone had a first or last name like Quillen.

"Yes. That's Quillen Shinn – Reverend Quillen Shinn."

"Who is Quillen Shinn?"

Carly began to tell Peter the story of Quillen Shinn. "He was a Universalist," she said. "He was a missionary. He traveled all over the country preaching about Universalism."

Peter remembered from his Religious Education classes that Universalists believed that *God is Love*, but he wondered what it had to do with Ferry Beach. Peter had not been to Ferry Beach before. He had never sung the most favorite song of campers at Ferry Beach, which was all about Quillen Shinn.

The song: *Quillen Shinn* is sung to the tune of *There is a Tavern in the Town.*

> 'Twas in the year of ninety-one, ninety-one,
> That Ferry Beach was first begun, first begun,
> When Quillen Shinn and his fourteen pioneers
> Insured their vision for the years.
>
> First they bought the grove for preaching,
> Then they saw the need for teaching,
> And achieved a brilliant conquest over
> Doubts and fears.
>
> CHORUS:
> Oh Shinn, O dear old Quillen Shinn, Quillen
> Shinn!
> To you we raise this grateful din, grateful din!
> We will lift your name
> To the Highest green pine tree
> And pledge, and pledge our loyalty.
>
> In bygone days the Boston Maine, Boston Maine,
> Puffed near the shore with dummy train, dummy
> train,
> And railroad men from far and roundabout
> Did gather here to roust and shout,
> But our fathers liked fish chowder,
> And our preachers shouted louder,
> 'Til they drove he dummy
> and the railroaders Out! CHORUS

Oh, once we had a pavilion, pavilion.
And it was one in a million, million,
And the darned old would always spring a leak
When brother Doe began to speak.
They were enterprising fellers.
For the folks all brought umbrellers
And the sermon moved along
Without a single break! CHORUS

The Belmont was a bowling hall, bowling hall.
And echoed with the thundering ball,
thundering ball!
For thus the blades of other happy days "Did
roll the idle hours away.
Then we silenced all the roarers,
But we got instead our snorers, "You can hear
them in the grove
Or, out in Saco Bay. CHORUS

There is no end to history, history,
But we will make no mystery, mystery,
That Rowland Hall and good old Underwood,
Show progress on the forward road.
So we beg you to remember
In the midst of next December
That we'll come again next summer
back to Ferry Beach. CHORUS

Carly told him about how Quillen Shinn was a circuit rider minister that went from town to town on horseback, preaching and spreading the word of Universalism. People called him the "Grasshopper Missionary," because he hopped from town to town.

Shinn also believed that Universalists needed a place to gather in the summer where lots of ministers could preach and people from all around could come to hear them. They set up large tents where their "summer meetings" took place for about 25 years. Then, Shinn bought an old hotel on Saco Bay, which is now Quillen. Over the years, other parts of Ferry Beach were purchased and built into the camp and conference center it is now.

"Wow!" said Peter. "How did you know all that?"

"Well, I've been coming to Ferry Beach since before I was born, so my mom tells me," said Carly shrugging as if to say that it wasn't any big idea. "I bet you don't know what a "teeny tiny" is either?"

Peter shook his head. Later, Carly bought him one at the Ferry Beach store. He picked chocolate. Carly had Moose Tracks, which is very popular in Maine.

"Hey, this is pretty cute!" Peter remarked about his tiny ice cream cone.

"Yep!" answered Carly in between licks. "And, it's the only place that has them!"

Peter loved the beach. Although it was early Spring and only the kids at his church were there, Peter fell in love with Ferry Beach. Most of his church friends had been coming for this weekend for years. It was their church's annual Ferry Beach Retreat.

Peter didn't want to go swimming, even though most of the other kids did. Instead, he spent his beach time picking up shells to add to his collection. He was also interested in the Ferry Beach Ecology School, which had displays in the Quillen lobby. He was fascinated with the natural world, especially sea life, which is probably why he had such a large collection of shells.

He wondered if Quillen Shinn would have also been an ecologist? He also wondered if it was the Universalist or the Unitarian part of being a UU (Unitarian Universalist) that made him feel so strong about the earth and all that lived on it.

He didn't have too much time to think about it, because Isaiah and Jeremy came running up to him. "It's time for the scavenger hunt!" they announced, pulling on him to go with them.

"Are you making puppets later?" they asked.

The three of them went running to get their papers for the scavenger hunt. Isaiah's group had won last year, so they had a bit of incentive to do good this year, as well. They started on the Quillen porch.

Peter read the first question, "What is the Red or 1st Principle?"

Isaiah said, "I know the answer to that!"

Peter looked in awe as Isaiah, blurted out, "That's *Respect All Beings*!"

Isaiah read the next question. The whole team took turns. They answered all the questions, which were the seven UU Principles by which UUs try to live their lives.

The rest of the questions and answers were:

What is the Violet or 7th Principle? Value our earth and all that lives upon it.

What is the Blue or 5th Principle? Believe in our ideas and act upon them.

What is orange or 2nd Principle? Offer Fair and Kind Treatment.

What is Indigo or the 6th Principle? Insist on peace, freedom and justice for all.

What is the green or 4th Principle? Grow by exploring ideas and values together.

What is the Yellow or 3rd Principle? Yearn to Learn throughout Life!

They took their paper and turned it in to Rev. Pat, who looked over the paper and smiled. "You got all the answers correct. Isaiah, didn't you win this last year?"

Isaiah beamed. It was his second year in a row to be on the winning team. And although there was a prize, which is a teeny tiny for each team member, the win was a since of accomplishment.

When Isaiah looked around the team, he saw that everyone was sporting big smiles, especially Peter!

"Are we making puppets?" asked Peter.

The rest of the team, answered in unison, "Yes!" The whole team ran to the DeWolfe Dining Room to make puppets. They all wanted to be in the talent show, so this was one way to be on stage without having to do anything but make a sock puppet.

EENY, MEENY, MINEY, MOE

written in 2009

Heather couldn't decide which *gender* she should pick on any given day. One day, she felt more male. Another day, she felt more female. But on some days neither gender seemed to fit.

When Heather got to college and went to work at Ferry Beach, a Unitarian Universalist camp and conference center, she shaved her head bald and pierced her nose. Some people wondered if she were girl or boy? And some days Heather wasn't sure herself. She had tried on both genders from time to time, but in the end she decided she was neither.

"Why do we have to have only two choices?" Heather asked. "I'd like to have a third category for something neutral, and I've been hearing others talk about *gender neutral.*"

"Why don't you pick like we did when we were kids coming here to camp!" suggested Kit, who loved the idea of choosing genders. He liked wearing skirts from time to time; he thought it might have been handed down from his Scottish relatives. Then he burst into a little rhythmic ditty that he and Heather had made up their first year at camp and changed the words, of course, to match the gender question: "Eeny, meeny, miney, moe, which gender should I pick today: male, female, gender neutral, this is how we UUs (Unitarian Universalists) choose. Rock, paper, scissors. Rock, paper, scissors. One, two, three, four, five little UUs (Unitarian Universalists) sitting on the sand watching all the waves coming in and going out. Male. Female. Gender Neutral. Female, Male, Gender Neutral. Gender Neutral, Male, Female. Female, Male, Gender Neutral." Touching their hands together, Female landed on Heather, then Gender Neutral for Kit, and the last one on Heather for Male.

"Looks like you're Male today. I'll be Gender Neutral!" Kit announced to Heather.

"Can I borrow your work boots?" asked Heather. "I feel like dressing very butch!"

Lynn who had not participated in their selection process, but had heard the whole thing said, "Sweet! I'm female."

They all went about their duties at camp dressed as their chosen *gender*. No one said anything. It wasn't too surprising to anyone, because it was a Unitarian Universalist camp. Since UUs believe in the *inherent worth and dignity of every person*, the camp often saw males dressed in skirts and girls in decidedly male attire.

An odd thing happened on the evening that Lynn, Kit and Heather had chosen their *gender identities* randomly, a boy enrolled in the kid's camp asked Kit, "So what are you supposed to be?"

Kit was used to answering straight forward, so he said, "I'm *gender neutral.*"

"Oh!" said the boy. "What's that?"

Kit had to go into a long explanation for the child and wondered if his answers were okay.

Heather had a somewhat similar experience. "Are you a lesbian?" asked a girl named, Ginger, who was enrolled in the Middle School camp.

Heather answered, "Not today. I'm a male."

"How did you get to choose?" asked Ginger curiously.

"Me and two of my friends, who are here working, did our usual routine for selecting what *gender* we would be," said Heather.

Naturally, that sparked some questions about how you are choosing and what was *gender identity* anyway. Heather answered all the girl's questions. However, Ginger was confused about *gender neutral.* So Heather explained further.

"If I chose to be *gender neutral,*" asked Ginger. "How would I dress? How should people address me? I mean, you can't say *he, she* or *it* for pronouns. What do you do?"

Heather eagerly and calmly explained, "There are some new pronouns to use for *Gender Neutral* people. You can say: *Zi* for *he* or *she;* and *Zir* for *her* or *him."*

"Oh!" said the girl. "Then there is already something to use? *Zi...Zir...*I think I like this *Gender Neutral* language...that's my choice, too! You see! I'm not really a girl or a boy. I feel more like something in between."

Heather and the girl talked for a long while. Heather answered all her questions. The girl had never been clear what her *gender identity* was, but she knew she didn't fit well as a boy or girl. For the first time, Ginger felt she understood her own body.

Heather, Lynn, and Kit talked about Ginger and her questions. Kit and Lynn urged Heather to share in a workshop about her ideas surrounding *gender issues* and talk about the *gender neutral* language in hopes that more *Trans* children and adults might understand what was happening to them. It also helped people stretch themselves around *gender diversity.*

Heather did. And over the rest of the summer, she found literally a hundred or more people to share about *gender-neutral* and how a third option should be available on all forms, birth certificates, etc.

When summer was over and the young adults returned to their homes in Massachusetts, they joined Mass Equality, which had worked to get equality for marriage passed and was now in the process of promoting *transgender equality* and supporting legislation to be passed to prevent hate crimes.

As for Ginger, she grew up to be *Trans.* She, too, became an activist to help get legislation passed that would help the entire LGBTQ (Lesbian, Gay, Bi-sexual, Trans [transgender and trans-sexual], Questioning community.

THE SAND FAIRIES

written at Ferry Beach 2004

Have you ever heard that the *Sandman* will come and give you dreams? There's even an old song about it. Lots of people say that it is the *Sandman* that comes to give you dreams, but that's not how it works...at least, it doesn't at Ferry Beach!

Ferry Beach is a special place; most folks that know about it say that it is! But few people know about the *Sand Fairies*. You see, where the *Sandman* may work in some places; here, there are *Sand Fairies*.

Where do they come from, you might ask? Well, it would seem logical that the *Sand Fairies* live in the *Sand Dunes*, but that's not where they are! When people play on the beach, make holes and fill them up, make beach art, create driftwood sculptures, or make sand castles, they bring the *Sand Fairies* to life. You probably won't see them, even though your actions bring them into our human world.

Some folks say they've seen the *Sand Fairies*, others aren't so sure. They exist just like the dunes do, and both are part of Ferry Beach. The high tides may sweep over the sand, but that doesn't bother the *Sand Fairies*. They make their home down into the sand, sometimes under the ocean's edge, and always down in the watery part of the sand.

The *Sand Fairies* are part of the *magic* of Ferry Beach. Most campers can tell you that *sand* and *magic* are part of Ferry Beach, but there are lots of explanations about both. It's true that sand is everywhere. One of my favorites include the showers! Nothing like walking on a bunch of grit while you're trying to get clean!

In spite of the fact that sand is everywhere, there are those who say, "There's no such thing as *magic*! And there's no such thing as *Sand Fairies*!"

Believe it or not, there are those who see the *magic* at Ferry Beach and know without a doubt that the Sand Fairies really exist. In fact, I've heard it said that every night when the *Kids for the Earth Camp* get in their pajamas and go to story time, a strange thing happens...

While the children are at story time, the *Sand Fairies* go to all the rooms and sprinkle *Sand Dreams* throughout the Quillen dorm rooms. Sometimes children notice *sand* in their rooms, or on their bed, or even sometimes on their pillow. That's when you know the *Sand Fairies* have brought you a dream or two.

However, the *magic* of Ferry Beach doesn't just happen for certain camps, it happens for all of them. So, all the people of all the ages and at every camp and even for vacationers, the *Sand Fairies* do their *magic*. It helps if you believe in the *Sand Fairies*! I've heard people comment about their *dreams*, and while that doesn't prove that the *Sand Fairies* exist...it doesn't hurt!

The next time you're at Ferry Beach, go down to the beach and make holes in the sand, see it through your *magical* lens, and watch for sand tracks wherever you are. The *Sand Fairies* may bring you a delightful dream!

SEEDS FOR PUMPKIN

written at Ferry Beach in 2006

Pumpkin was a girl about 11 years old. Pumpkin was her special name that only her Grandmother and Mommas called her. Her real name, the one she used at school, was Josephine Heidi McBray.

Pumpkin felt very special, because she had two mothers and a grandmother who lived with her and cared for her. Her Grandmother loved gardening and working in the dirt, which pleased Pumpkin, because she, too, enjoyed playing in the dirt. When she had been younger, making mud pies was one of her favorite things to do. It was messy, but she didn't care. She liked getting covered in mud and dirt. She liked the way the earth smelled and how the leaves smelled in the fall when she raked them together and jumped on them. She even liked the compost heap, except for all the critters that seemed to scurry out when one of her moms or grandmother turned the compost, which meant they shoveled and mixed the compost to mix in the new leaves or cuttings or whatever natural substance was being added to the compost.

Momma L whose name was Linda liked planting bulbs. Momma K whose name was Katherine and was her birth mother liked potted plants best. And Grandmother, who was her Momma K's mother, loved garden plants. And with Grandmother, Pumpkin had planted pumpkin seeds every summer she could remember. Now, the pumpkins were growing large and plump and ready to pick. This was Pumpkin's favorite time of year, because, of course, with a nickname of Pumpkin, you just about had to like pumpkins. And as it happened, Pumpkin liked pumpkin bread, pumpkin pancakes, pumpkin pie, pumpkin fudge, pumpkin jelly, and toasted pumpkin seeds. She even liked the color pumpkin, which was the color of her room. And so, it was a joyful time to go out and pick the pumpkins off the vines.

Grandmother and Pumpkin got the wheelbarrow out of the shed and wheeled it over to the garden where the pumpkins were fat and orange in the bright autumn sun. Pumpkin thought that this day was the best day of the year. There were 30 pumpkins in Grandmother's pumpkin patch. And all of them were beautiful to Pumpkin. When they wheeled their last bunch to the porch, Momma L and Momma K came out to help do the sorting.

Momma L said, "Pumpkin, this looks like a good jack-o-lantern. Shall we save it for our special pumpkin ceremony?"

"Yes!" said Pumpkin very excited at the thought of their yearly pumpkin ceremony that she had almost forgotten until that moment.

Momma K picked out about six or seven pumpkins for making pies. She kept switching the last one around, because she couldn't make up her mind, which made Pumpkin laugh.

Grandmother picked out three pumpkins and put them to the side. "What are these for?" asked Pumpkin.

"Seeds," said Grandmother.

"To toast?" said Pumpkin, clapping her hands together.

"No," said Grandmother," this year will be a special Pumpkin ceremony with seeds, because this year you have turned eleven, which is a special year in every girl's life."

"It is?" Pumpkin questioned with a puzzled look on her face.

"It is!" said Grandmother without explaining more.

When all the pumpkins had been designated for one thing or another the piles were labeled and put into appropriate-sized baskets and placed in the cupboard for storage.

The Mommas went about making their evening meal with corn and beans and tomatoes still fresh from the garden. But when the meal was completed, Pumpkin knew it was the special Pumpkin Ceremony time.

Momma L brought out the pumpkin designated for being a jack-o-lantern. Momma K got out the newspaper and spread it on the table. Grandmother got the special pumpkin carving knife. And they all worked together removing the juicy pumpkin part and leaving in just the right amount. Pumpkin scraped all the seeds out. And finally, their work of art was complete: Jack-O-Lantern had just the right sort of smile and best shaped eyes. The candle was placed inside. And all the pumpkin had been cleaned up, saving seeds and pumpkin fruit pulp to use later.

They all went outside and placed the Jack-O-Lantern on its traditional post. The candle was lit. And Momma L began to recite her traditional poem:

> *Pumpkin, pumpkin*
> *big and round*
> *I'm glad you grow*
> *upon the ground.*
>
> *I'm glad you don't*
> *grow in a tree*
> *for then you might*
> *fall down on me.*

Pumpkin laughed like she did each year, because she knew pumpkins grew on vines not on trees.

And Momma K told her traditional story:

> *On the day you were born, it was Pumpkin Ceremony day – the day we harvested the pumpkins. You were born here at home with just us three and precisely at three o'clock! You were small and sort of orange that's why we call you Pumpkin. Other babies are wrinkly and pink, but not our precious Pumpkin. We put you under the sun lamp to keep you warm and snug. We carved our Jack-O-Lantern and lit the candle. Momma L read her poem. I held you in my arms and Grandmother fed me pumpkin bread. On the day you were born, it was Pumpkin Ceremony day.*

"And today," Grandmother said, "you are eleven years old. It's a special sort of time in every girl's life. When you are eleven you aren't ten anymore and you aren't quite twelve, which everyone knows means you're almost grown. So this is the year that we must celebrate you well. And here it is on Pumpkin Ceremony day..."

Momma L brought out the three special pumpkins. Grandmother brought out a large cutting knife. Momma L and Momma K and Grandmother all held their pumpkins in front of their Pumpkin.

Momma K said, "Let the seeds from this pumpkin open your mind and grow the thoughts that will help lead your way through the rest of your life."

She took the knife and sliced the pumpkin revealing its seeds.

Momma L said, "Let the seeds from this pumpkin open your eyes and help you see the love in every seed and soul."

She took the knife and sliced the pumpkin revealing its seeds.

Grandmother said, "Let the seeds from this pumpkin open your mouth and voice so that you might always voice the truth."

She took the knife and sliced the pumpkin revealing its seeds.

Each of the women picked out seeds from the pumpkins and put them into a pouch that Grandmother had sewn for Pumpkin.

Together, the women said, "May the seeds in this pouch remind you of your Pumpkin years and shine light upon all you do."

They placed the pouch around her neck. Pumpkin hugged her Grandmother and her Momma L and her Momma K. And she knew it really was the best Pumpkin Celebration Day yet.

MUSCA AND THE CHALICE

idea conceived at Ferry Beach 2010

Charlie peeked into the Children's Chapel. When he saw Musca, he shut the door and ran out to find some of his friends. "There's a DRAGON in the Chapel!"

Lilly and Tyler and Justin simultaneously screamed, "A DRAGON!" Then the three ran toward the Chapel to look. Sure enough! There was a Dragon in the Chapel. It wasn't Charlie's imagination or one of his jokes; it was a real live DRAGON.

The three of them went running into Rev. Pat's office to announce that there was a Dragon in the Chapel. Rev. Pat said, "Yes, there is! Isn't it exciting?"

The three friends went to find Charlie to tell him, but they ran into more and more of the children at their church. Naturally, they had to tell them all that there was a Dragon in their Chapel. Charlie was at the entrance to their religious education wing also announcing that there was a Dragon in their Chapel.

As the morning ticked away, the Chapel became packed! Even some of the older children and youth went to Children's Chapel, because they wanted to know why the Dragon was in their Chapel. Charlie found a seat near the front of the Chapel along with Tyler, Lily, and Justin.

In what seemed like an eternity to Charlie, Rev. Pat finally entered the Chapel and made her way to the small pulpit that graced the front of the Children's Chapel. "Today, we are going to talk about *The Mystery that Some People Call God*. And the reason that I've brought Musca (Moo-skah) here…" she gestured to Musca, "is that Dragons are known for their great wisdom and mystical knowledge."

A hand went up in the crowded room, but Rev. Pat took her time before asking its recipient to ask their question.

"Aren't Dragons mythological characters? Uh…Um…Is Musca really a Dragon?"

Musca turned to face the children and youth. He stood and his head nearly hit the ceiling. A lot of jaws dropped in disbelief of his enormity. He was huge. Somehow while he was sitting or squatting or whatever dragons do, he seemed smaller – more the size of a human adult, which to some of the smaller children seemed fairly large, anyway. Now, he was a giant!

There was a silence that clouded over the children and youth in the Chapel that day. It was so thick that Charlie thought he needed to crack it by karate chopping it. He controlled his urges, because he knew that was not proper behavior for the Children's Chapel.

Musca's size seemed to loom larger than life. It seemed to fill all the empty space in the room, which oddly felt like Musca not only was in front of the group but also in and around every-thing and every-one.

His voice was low and quiet yet familiar in some way. Charlie thought of all the people in his life that made him feel safe, comfortable, and belonging to something greater than himself. "Yes!" he said in his head. "That's exactly how Dragons feel to me, like my Great Aunt Charlotte or Uncle Bernard."

Musca smiled. Charlie noticed. Then he understood, "Musca did not need to use his voice to communicate." That revelation was Charlie's alone, or, at least Charlie thought so.

The Dragon pulled out some glasses. At first, Charlie thought they were reading glasses, but at closer examination, Charlie realized that they created a protective barrier for Musca.

"I'm real!" Musca said quietly.

Rev. Pat said, "Let's light our Chalice."

Before anyone could say anything, Musca shot a flame out of his mouth and lit the Chalice! Some of the girls gasped. Most of the boys rolled their eyes. Charlie whispered, "Cool!" to Tyler. "Do you think he'll talk to us after Church?"

"What do you think, our Flaming Chalice, Fire Breathing Dragons like Musca, and the Mystery that Some People Call God all have in common?" Rev. Pat asked.

Charlie raised his hand.

"Charlie," Rev. Pat said.

"Ummmm...well, Flaming Chalices and Fire Breathing Dragons have fire in common."

"Good!" said Rev. Pat. "And the *Mystery that Some People Call God?*"

Charlie shook his head and shrugged his shoulders.

"Okay." Rev. Pat said. "Who else has an idea?"

Jonah said, "Well, God is supposed to be BIG and Dragons are BIG!"

"That's an interesting idea, Jonah, but I was looking for something more...uh...a little more spiritual," Rev. Pat said.

Lily half-heartedly raised her hand. Rev. Pat called on her. "Dragons are supposed to be rich in wealth and wisdom. I didn't think they were real, though!"

"As you can see; Musca is real," continued Rev. Pat. "Throughout history, dragons have been magical and mystical creatures and appeared in much of the mythology of most cultures."

"In some cultures," Musca began in a very quiet tone, which contrasted his giant size. "We've actually been considered like God...or that *Mystery that Some People Call God*. You see, my species has been around for a very long time. We live best in literature, mostly fantasy. That's probably why you all wondered if I was real! The Dragon Slayers may have killed off a lot of us, but we still exist. We just aren't very visible. We live mostly deep in the caverns of the earth.

"Would you believe that God lives down in the belly of the earth with us Dragons? But God also lives here in the Chapel, and in each of you? God doesn't just live on this earth and down in the planetary gut, God is the earth. God is the air we breathe and the plants and trees, and the animals, birds, fish, and insects.

Charlie heard what Musca was saying, but at the same time felt himself transplanted into a different time. Musca was there with him and was talking to him: "Charlie, you must grab the shield!"

"What shield?" Charlie cried.

"The big, round one with the Dragon on it." Musca said calmly.

Charlie felt panicked as warriors on horses pounded closer and closer to him. "What do I do?"

"Shield. Sword." Musca's voice was strong and calm.

Charlie was so confused, "But...but..."

"Sword. Shield."

As Charlie picked up the sword, it felt heavier than he imagined. Then, he grabbed the shield, which weighted him down even more. The warriors were so close; he could feel the hot breath of the horses all around him. And then like magic, they disappeared into a cloud of dust.

Charlie coughed, looked around in disbelief, and asked Musca, "What happened?"

"You invoked the magic of the Dragon." There was a long pause, then Musca continued, "*The Mystery that Some People Call God.*"

"So God? Or the Dragon? Saved me?" Charlie asked.

"Neither!" Musca explained.

"I don't understand," said Charlie feeling even more confused and was wondering if he was dreaming or something, because everything seemed all muddled in his head.

"The power and magic of the Dragon and the *Mystery that Some People Call God* is in you, Charlie. It's always been there!"

"Where did the Chapel go?" Charlie asked.

"We're still in it. You just transported us into ancient times."

"I did?"

"Yes, Charlie. You have a job to do."

"I do?"

"You need to take up the instruments, like the sword and the shield, to defend your world from the Dragon Slayers."

"I can barely pick up the sword or the shield!"

"Charlie, your world is shifting. There are those who embrace the Dark; and those that have moved too far to the right of Light that they, too, are in the Dark. They don't know they have slipped into the Dark. They believe they are in the right and everyone else is not."

"But Musca, I'm just a kid!"

"And I'm just a Dragon."

"But you can see what needs to be done, so why can't you do it?"

"It is not my time to take up the sword and shield, Charlie. It is yours."

"But I don't know what to do."

"You know more than you think you do. And there are those who will help you, like Rev. Pat."

"But do what?"

"Be the voice of the Light, Charlie. You wouldn't have come here, if this wasn't your life's purpose.

You need to rely on the *Mystery that Some People Call God* that lives within your Soul. It is your generation that will determine how Earth will be. It can be the Dark planet or stand for the Light that radiates from within you. You do not have to do this alone. Look around at your friends! They, too, will take up that sword and shield to protect your world from sliding into the Darkness."

"Okay, Musca. Will you help, too?"

"Yes, Charlie, I will."

When Musca and Charlie returned to Charlie's time in the Chapel, the Children's Chapel was just ending. Lilly turned to him, "Charlie, I will help!"

Charlie was still a bit confused about what he was to do. But, somehow, knowing that Lilly would help him in his quest made him feel that it was all doable...whatever it was that he needed to do.

In the years that followed, Charlie learned a lot about who he was and the *Mystery that Some People Call God*. He learned many things that were foreign to him like the sword and shield that he had picked up at Musca's urging.

Charlie grew up to be a minister with a strong history of working for justice. Musca was Charlie's trusted advisor. Lilly also became a minister, together, they spoke to children and adults all around the globe.

ABOUT THE AUTHOR

Connie Dunn

Photo by Andy Heller

Connie Dunn, owner of Nature Woman Wisdom and Publish with Connie, is an author, speaker and educator. Her specialty is indie publishing. She has taught writing, freelance writing, religious education, and a variety of creativity workshops.

She has been writing all her life. She has written about 30 books, screen plays, and curricula.

She spent about 25 years as a Religious Educator, where she wrote a *Story for All Ages* just about every week to match the minister's message. In this collection, she put together stories that she told, wrote, or set at Ferry Beach.

Connie has a bachelor's degree in Marketing and Small Business Management. She spent more than 20 years as freelance writer and had a regular column in such publications as *The Dallas Morning*

News. This column earned her an award from the SBA for her work with Home-Based Businesses.

A native of Texas, she now lives in Franklin, Massachusetts, with her wife, Joyce, and their tiny Chihuahua, Rusty, and plus-size cat, Sophie.

She and Joyce are regulars at Ferry Beach, where they attend *In the Company of Women*, which is a week-long camp for women.

Other Books Written by Connie Dunn

A Spider, Some Thread, and a Labyrinth Walk
A-Spider-Some-Thread-and-a-Labyrinth-Walk.com

Book Writing: Fuzzy About Where to Start?
BookWriting-FuzzyAboutWhereToStart.com

Goddess Rituals: Reclaiming Our Ancient Spiritual Heritage
GoddessRituals.webs.com

Miss Odell: The Privileges of Being Present for the End of Her Life - A Reality Book on Elder Care
MissOdell-RealityBook.com

Press Releases Made Easy
Press-Releases-Made-Easy.com

The Most Magical, Awesome, Delicate Creature of All
The-Most-Magical-Awesome-Delicate-Creature-of-All.com

The Real Story of the Dumpty Family
therealstoryofthedumptyfamily.com

Trees: Peaceful and Personal Meditational Poems
Trees-Meditative.com

Zoe
zoe-the-book.com